Foreword for Parents

A growth mindset is inherent in every child. There would be no development otherwise. When they are newborn and toddlers, children learn to do things without thinking, and relentlessly pursue taks, and persevere, until they master them.

But as they grow up, older kids start to analyse the world around them, and their thinking brain starts to get in the way. Children start to doubt themselves and put limits on themselves.

It's our job as parents to guide children and to instil in them the belief that, just like toddlers, they can achieve any goal they work at. And it's our job to nurture in them a lifelong thirst for learning that will help them acquire the skills they need to keep a growth mindset into adulthood.

As parents, we've read about the benefits of a growth mindset - the tool set of flexibility and adaptability skills that help children and adults navigate life successfully. But how do we help develop this mindset in our children?

The Weekly Success Journal is a guided journal designed to help children realise that they already possess the skills they need to foster a growth mindset. They just need to practice these skills on a daily basis and in every activity.

The journal is developed around the simple premise that kids naturally use a growth mindset towards the things they want to learn, like learning to ride a bike. But they usually close up that positive mindset when it comes to things they perceive as unpleasant - such as learning to read or doing math.

By utilising this prompt journal on a regular basis, kids will begin to internalise the idea that anything can be learnt and that goals are achievable when broken down into small steps.

About this journal:

This journal is divided into 52 weekly sections, with some fun diversions in between, and allows kids to write down their weekly goals, break them down into tasks, and follow their success over time.

My name is _____ But I go by _____

I'm really good at _____ and _____

My best friend is _____

My best friend is really good at _____

I have another friend who is really good at _____

When I grown up I want to be _____

Because _____

To be that, I need to be able to do these 4 things (at least):

_____   _____

_____   _____

But secretly, I also want to be _____

Because _____

This is what I need to know to be that _____

_____

The things I can do better than any kid I know are _____

_____

My friends want to be able to do this like me _____

_____

Dream Big

Let's start big!

Out of everything in the world, what is the one thing that you really want to know how to do (that you don't already know how to do)? What is your biggest dream? Don't worry if you can't achieve it right now. Just write it down.

_____
_____
_____
_____
_____

Can you draw it? What would you look like achieving it?

Now let's go really small! How do you get to that big dream?

Are there any things you need to learn how to do?

_____
_____
_____

Do you need to take any special courses? What do you think they are called?

_____
_____
_____

Are there any books you can read? What are some titles, do you think?

_____
_____
_____

Are there people you can talk to that can give you more information about it?

_____
_____
_____

And now, make a list of **all** the things you want to learn how to do! Every single last one of them, even the smallest ones! (use lots of different colors, if you want)

That's a great list! Good for you for having so many interests!

Things we want to learn to do are called **goals**. Grownups talk about **achieving** goals. That's another way of saying that you have to **take small steps** (tasks) to get to your goal.

There are **short-terms goals** - like eating a whole ice cream before it starts melting. And **long-term goals** - like trying every flavor of ice cream at the store.

Short term goals can be achieved in a **few steps** in a **short time**.
But long-term goals **take time** and **many steps**. They take patience, but the rewards are fantastic! Think of all that ice cream!

Let's say you wanted to learn how to fly a plane, what steps would you have to take in order to do it? Make a list:

_____

_____

_____

Now put those steps in order. What do you need to learn first? What comes last?

_____   _____

_____   _____

_____   _____

Do you know what skills are? ☐ Yes ☐ No

Can you do any of the following?

☐ Read ☐ Sing ☐ Ride a bike

☐ Write ☐ Ski ☐ Play an instrument

☐ Do math ☐ Play computer games ☐ Build with Lego

☐ Draw or paint ☐ Swim ☐ Play a team sport

Are you really good at some of these? Which ones?
_____
_____
_____

Are you good at some other things as well? What are they?
_____
_____
_____

Being able to do something is called a **skill**.

Now that you know for sure what skills are, list 3 skills you are most proud of:

1.

2.

3.

How did you get so good at these skills?

☐ Practice   ☐ I was born that way   ☐ Magic

☐ Read it in a book   ☐ Watched on TV   ☐ I ate something?

Chances are, one of the main reasons you got good at your top 3 skills is because you **practiced**.

Take one of your favorite skills above. How did you get so good at it?

_____

_____

_____

Did it take a long time to learn? How long did you practice?

_____

_____

You see, you already know that to achieve a goal you have to take steps towards it and practice.
Let's take that and apply it to your whole year ahead!

My plan for being awesome

My plan for the week

☆ Things that I plan to accomplish this week (my short-term goals):
_____
_____
_____

This is what I need to do to achieve my goals this week:
_____
_____
_____
_____

☆ The long-term goals that I'll work on this week are:
_____
_____
_____

This is what I need to do to work towards them:
_____
_____
_____
_____

☆ This week I'll keep trying to get better at _____ and work on _____
_____
_____
_____

Pick the goal you want to achieve the most this week and write it here:

Draw one of your goals for this week. Draw what you look like achieving it:

☆ **Last week in review:**

What were my successes? What goals did I achieve? What can I learn from my successes?

_____
_____

Any mistakes? What can I do differently next time? Can I talk to anyone and ask them questions about how to do better next time (find our their secrets to success)?

_____
_____

Color a star for each goal you achieved last week and write the name of the goal in (draw more stars if you need to):

My plan for the week

☆ Things that I plan to accomplish this week (my short-term goals):
_____
_____
_____

This is what I need to do to achieve my goals this week:
_____
_____
_____
_____

☆ The long-term goals that I'll work on this week are:
_____
_____
_____

This is what I need to do to work towards them:
_____
_____
_____
_____

☆ This week I'll keep trying to get better at _____ and work on _____
_____
_____

Pick the goal you want to achieve the most this week and write it here:

Draw one of your goals for this week. Draw what you look like achieving it:

☆ **Last week in review:**

What were my successes? What goals did I achieve? What can I learn from my successes?

_____

_____

Any mistakes? What can I do differently next time? Can I talk to anyone and ask them questions about how to do better next time (find our their secrets to success)?

_____

_____

Color a star for each goal you achieved last week and write the name of the goal in (draw more stars if you need to):

My plan for the week

☆ Things that I plan to accomplish this week (my short-term goals):

_____
_____
_____

This is what I need to do to achieve my goals this week:

_____
_____
_____
_____

☆ The long-term goals that I'll work on this week are:

_____
_____
_____

This is what I need to do to work towards them:

_____
_____
_____

☆ This week I'll keep trying to get better at _____ and work on _____

_____
_____

Pick the goal you want to achieve the most this week and write it here:

Draw one of your goals for this week. Draw what you look like achieving it:

☆ Last week in review:

What were my successes? What goals did I achieve? What can I learn from my successes?
_____
_____

Any mistakes? What can I do differently next time? Can I talk to anyone and ask them questions about how to do better next time (find our their secrets to success)?
_____
_____

Color a star for each goal you achieved last week and write the name of the goal in (draw more stars if you need to):

My plan for the week

☆ Things that I plan to accomplish this week (my short-term goals):
_____
_____
_____

This is what I need to do to achieve my goals this week:
_____
_____
_____
_____

☆ The long-term goals that I'll work on this week are:
_____
_____
_____

This is what I need to do to work towards them:
_____
_____
_____
_____

☆ This week I'll keep trying to get better at _____ and work on _____
_____
_____

Pick the goal you want to achieve the most this week and write it here:

Draw one of your goals for this week. Draw what you look like achieving it:

☆ **Last week in review:**

What were my successes? What goals did I achieve? What can I learn from my successes?

_____

_____

Any mistakes? What can I do differently next time? Can I talk to anyone and ask them questions about how to do better next time (find our their secrets to success)?

_____

_____

Color a star for each goal you achieved last week and write the name of the goal in (draw more stars if you need to):

My plan for the week

☆ Things that I plan to accomplish this week (my short-term goals):
_____
_____
_____

This is what I need to do to achieve my goals this week:
_____
_____
_____
_____

☆ The long-term goals that I'll work on this week are:
_____
_____
_____

This is what I need to do to work towards them:
_____
_____
_____
_____

☆ This week I'll keep trying to get better at _____ and work on _____
_____
_____
_____

Pick the goal you want to achieve the most this week and write it here:

Draw one of your goals for this week. Draw what you look like achieving it:

☆ Last week in review:

What were my successes? What goals did I achieve? What can I learn from my successes?

_____
_____

Any mistakes? What can I do differently next time? Can I talk to anyone and ask them questions about how to do better next time (find our their secrets to success)?

_____
_____

Color a star for each goal you achieved last week and write the name of the goal in (draw more stars if you need to):

My plan for the week

☆ Things that I plan to accomplish this week (my short-term goals):
_____
_____
_____

This is what I need to do to achieve my goals this week:
_____
_____
_____
_____

☆ The long-term goals that I'll work on this week are:
_____
_____
_____

This is what I need to do to work towards them:
_____
_____
_____
_____

☆ This week I'll keep trying to get better at _____ and work on _____
_____
_____

Pick the goal you want to achieve the most this week and write it here:

Draw one of your goals for this week. Draw what you look like achieving it:

☆ **Last week in review:**

What were my successes? What goals did I achieve? What can I learn from my successes?
_____
_____

Any mistakes? What can I do differently next time? Can I talk to anyone and ask them questions about how to do better next time (find our their secrets to success)?
_____
_____

Color a star for each goal you achieved last week and write the name of the goal in (draw more stars if you need to):

Let's play a game! Pretend you are a **secret spy**.

What is your secret spy name? _____

What are your top 3 special secret spy skills?

      1.

      2.

      3.

What is your mission?
_____
_____
_____

What is your favorite spy tool? _____

What does it do? _____
_____

Draw it.

Draw what you would look like as a secret spy.

My plan for the week

☆ Things that I plan to accomplish this week (my short-term goals):
_____
_____
_____

This is what I need to do to achieve my goals this week:
_____
_____
_____
_____

☆ The long-term goals that I'll work on this week are:
_____
_____
_____

This is what I need to do to work towards them:
_____
_____
_____
_____

☆ This week I'll keep trying to get better at _____ and work on _____
_____
_____

Pick the goal you want to achieve the most this week and write it here:

Draw one of your goals for this week. Draw what you look like achieving it:

☆ **Last week in review:**

What were my successes? What goals did I achieve? What can I learn from my successes?

_____

_____

Any mistakes? What can I do differently next time? Can I talk to anyone and ask them questions about how to do better next time (find our their secrets to success)?

_____

_____

Color a star for each goal you achieved last week and write the name of the goal in (draw more stars if you need to):

My plan for the week

☆ Things that I plan to accomplish this week (my short-term goals):
_____
_____
_____

This is what I need to do to achieve my goals this week:
_____
_____
_____
_____

☆ The long-term goals that I'll work on this week are:
_____
_____
_____

This is what I need to do to work towards them:
_____
_____
_____

☆ This week I'll keep trying to get better at _____ and work on _____
_____
_____

Pick the goal you want to achieve the most this week and write it here:

Draw one of your goals for this week. Draw what you look like achieving it:

☆ **Last week in review:**

What were my successes? What goals did I achieve? What can I learn from my successes?

_____
_____

Any mistakes? What can I do differently next time? Can I talk to anyone and ask them questions about how to do better next time (find our their secrets to success)?

_____
_____

Color a star for each goal you achieved last week and write the name of the goal in (draw more stars if you need to):

My plan for the week

☆ Things that I plan to accomplish this week (my short-term goals):
_____
_____
_____
_____

This is what I need to do to achieve my goals this week:
_____
_____
_____
_____

☆ The long-term goals that I'll work on this week are:
_____
_____
_____
_____

This is what I need to do to work towards them:
_____
_____
_____
_____

☆ This week I'll keep trying to get better at _____ and work on _____
_____
_____
_____

Pick the goal you want to achieve the most this week and write it here:

Draw one of your goals for this week. Draw what you look like achieving it:

☆ **Last week in review:**

What were my successes? What goals did I achieve? What can I learn from my successes?

_____
_____

Any mistakes? What can I do differently next time? Can I talk to anyone and ask them questions about how to do better next time (find our their secrets to success)?

_____
_____

Color a star for each goal you achieved last week and write the name of the goal in (draw more stars if you need to):

My plan for the week

☆ Things that I plan to accomplish this week (my short-term goals):
_____
_____
_____

This is what I need to do to achieve my goals this week:
_____
_____
_____
_____

☆ The long-term goals that I'll work on this week are:
_____
_____
_____

This is what I need to do to work towards them:
_____
_____
_____
_____

☆ This week I'll keep trying to get better at _____ and work on _____
_____
_____

Pick the goal you want to achieve the most this week and write it here:

Draw one of your goals for this week. Draw what you look like achieving it:

☆ Last week in review:

What were my successes? What goals did I achieve? What can I learn from my successes?

_____
_____

Any mistakes? What can I do differently next time? Can I talk to anyone and ask them questions about how to do better next time (find our their secrets to success)?

_____
_____

Color a star for each goal you achieved last week and write the name of the goal in (draw more stars if you need to):

My plan for the week

☆ Things that I plan to accomplish this week (my short-term goals):
_____
_____
_____

This is what I need to do to achieve my goals this week:
_____
_____
_____
_____

☆ The long-term goals that I'll work on this week are:
_____
_____
_____

This is what I need to do to work towards them:
_____
_____
_____

☆ This week I'll keep trying to get better at _____ and work on _____
_____
_____

Pick the goal you want to achieve the most this week and write it here:

Draw one of your goals for this week. Draw what you look like achieving it:

☆ **Last week in review:**

What were my successes? What goals did I achieve? What can I learn from my successes?

_____
_____

Any mistakes? What can I do differently next time? Can I talk to anyone and ask them questions about how to do better next time (find our their secrets to success)?

_____
_____

Color a star for each goal you achieved last week and write the name of the goal in (draw more stars if you need to):

My plan for the week

☆ Things that I plan to accomplish this week (my short-term goals):
_____
_____
_____

This is what I need to do to achieve my goals this week:
_____
_____
_____
_____

☆ The long-term goals that I'll work on this week are:
_____
_____
_____

This is what I need to do to work towards them:
_____
_____
_____
_____

☆ This week I'll keep trying to get better at _____ and work on _____
_____
_____
_____

Pick the goal you want to achieve the most this week and write it here:

Draw one of your goals for this week. Draw what you look like achieving it:

☆ **Last week in review:**

What were my successes? What goals did I achieve? What can I learn from my successes?

_____
_____

Any mistakes? What can I do differently next time? Can I talk to anyone and ask them questions about how to do better next time (find our their secrets to success)?

_____
_____

Color a star for each goal you achieved last week and write the name of the goal in (draw more stars if you need to):

Let's play a game! Today you're an **ice cream inventor**.

What new ice cream flavor do you want to invent? _____

Does this new ice cream taste good?   ☐ Yes   ☐ No

What's in it?

_____   _____

_____   _____

_____   _____

Give this new flavor a great name. Something that will make everyone curious and want to try it :

What color is it? Can you invent a new color name for it as well?
_____
_____

What does it taste like?
_____
_____

Draw and decorate an ice cream sundae made with your new ice cream flavor. Draw all the toppings you want to put on it.

My plan for the week

☆ Things that I plan to accomplish this week (my short-term goals):
_____
_____
_____

This is what I need to do to achieve my goals this week:
_____
_____
_____
_____

☆ The long-term goals that I'll work on this week are:
_____
_____
_____

This is what I need to do to work towards them:
_____
_____
_____
_____

☆ This week I'll keep trying to get better at _____ and work on _____
_____
_____

Pick the goal you want to achieve the most this week and write it here:

Draw one of your goals for this week. Draw what you look like achieving it:

☆ Last week in review:

What were my successes? What goals did I achieve? What can I learn from my successes?

_____

_____

Any mistakes? What can I do differently next time? Can I talk to anyone and ask them questions about how to do better next time (find our their secrets to success)?

_____

_____

Color a star for each goal you achieved last week and write the name of the goal in (draw more stars if you need to):

My plan for the week

☆ Things that I plan to accomplish this week (my short-term goals):
_____
_____
_____

This is what I need to do to achieve my goals this week:
_____
_____
_____
_____

☆ The long-term goals that I'll work on this week are:
_____
_____
_____

This is what I need to do to work towards them:
_____
_____
_____

☆ This week I'll keep trying to get better at _____ and work on _____
_____
_____

Pick the goal you want to achieve the most this week and write it here:

Draw one of your goals for this week. Draw what you look like achieving it:

☆ Last week in review:

What were my successes? What goals did I achieve? What can I learn from my successes?

_____
_____

Any mistakes? What can I do differently next time? Can I talk to anyone and ask them questions about how to do better next time (find our their secrets to success)?

_____
_____

Color a star for each goal you achieved last week and write the name of the goal in (draw more stars if you need to):

My plan for the week

☆ Things that I plan to accomplish this week (my short-term goals):
_____
_____
_____

This is what I need to do to achieve my goals this week:
_____
_____
_____
_____

☆ The long-term goals that I'll work on this week are:
_____
_____
_____

This is what I need to do to work towards them:
_____
_____
_____

☆ This week I'll keep trying to get better at _____ and work on _____
_____
_____

Pick the goal you want to achieve the most this week and write it here:

Draw one of your goals for this week. Draw what you look like achieving it:

☆ **Last week in review:**

What were my successes? What goals did I achieve? What can I learn from my successes?

_____

_____

Any mistakes? What can I do differently next time? Can I talk to anyone and ask them questions about how to do better next time (find our their secrets to success)?

_____

_____

Color a star for each goal you achieved last week and write the name of the goal in (draw more stars if you need to):

My plan for the week

☆ Things that I plan to accomplish this week (my short-term goals):
___
___
___

This is what I need to do to achieve my goals this week:
___
___
___
___

☆ The long-term goals that I'll work on this week are:
___
___
___

This is what I need to do to work towards them:
___
___
___

☆ This week I'll keep trying to get better at _____ and work on _____
___
___

Pick the goal you want to achieve the most this week and write it here:

Draw one of your goals for this week. Draw what you look like achieving it:

☆ Last week in review:

What were my successes? What goals did I achieve? What can I learn from my successes?
_____
_____

Any mistakes? What can I do differently next time? Can I talk to anyone and ask them questions about how to do better next time (find our their secrets to success)?
_____
_____

Color a star for each goal you achieved last week and write the name of the goal in (draw more stars if you need to):

My plan for the week

☆ Things that I plan to accomplish this week (my short-term goals):
___
___
___

This is what I need to do to achieve my goals this week:
___
___
___
___

☆ The long-term goals that I'll work on this week are:
___
___
___

This is what I need to do to work towards them:
___
___
___

☆ This week I'll keep trying to get better at _____ and work on _____
___
___

Pick the goal you want to achieve the most this week and write it here:

Draw one of your goals for this week. Draw what you look like achieving it:

☆ **Last week in review:**

What were my successes? What goals did I achieve? What can I learn from my successes?

_____
_____

Any mistakes? What can I do differently next time? Can I talk to anyone and ask them questions about how to do better next time (find our their secrets to success)?

_____
_____

Color a star for each goal you achieved last week and write the name of the goal in (draw more stars if you need to):

My plan for the week

☆ Things that I plan to accomplish this week (my short-term goals):
_____
_____
_____

This is what I need to do to achieve my goals this week:
_____
_____
_____
_____

☆ The long-term goals that I'll work on this week are:
_____
_____
_____

This is what I need to do to work towards them:
_____
_____
_____
_____

☆ This week I'll keep trying to get better at _____ and work on _____
_____
_____

Pick the goal you want to achieve the most this week and write it here:

Draw one of your goals for this week. Draw what you look like achieving it:

☆ Last week in review:

What were my successes? What goals did I achieve? What can I learn from my successes?

_____
_____

Any mistakes? What can I do differently next time? Can I talk to anyone and ask them questions about how to do better next time (find our their secrets to success)?

_____
_____

Color a star for each goal you achieved last week and write the name of the goal in (draw more stars if you need to):

Let's play a game!

If you could invent a **game**, what would it be?

☐ Board Game   ☐ Computer Game

☐ Card Game   ☐ Something else

What's the name of your game?

What are the rules of your game?

_____   _____

_____   _____

_____   _____

How do you win at this game? Or is it a cooperative game?

_____

_____

How many people can play it at the same time? _____

What age do you have to be to play it? _____ to _____

Draw what your game looks like. Draw the game box. Draw the game pieces or cards (if you have those). Or draw the characters.

My plan for the week

☆ Things that I plan to accomplish this week (my short-term goals):
_____
_____
_____

This is what I need to do to achieve my goals this week:
_____
_____
_____
_____

☆ The long-term goals that I'll work on this week are:
_____
_____
_____

This is what I need to do to work towards them:
_____
_____
_____
_____

☆ This week I'll keep trying to get better at _____ and work on _____
_____
_____

Pick the goal you want to achieve the most this week and write it here:

Draw one of your goals for this week. Draw what you look like achieving it:

☆ **Last week in review:**

What were my successes? What goals did I achieve? What can I learn from my successes?

_____

_____

Any mistakes? What can I do differently next time? Can I talk to anyone and ask them questions about how to do better next time (find our their secrets to success)?

_____

_____

Color a star for each goal you achieved last week and write the name of the goal in (draw more stars if you need to):

My plan for the week

☆ Things that I plan to accomplish this week (my short-term goals):
___
___
___

This is what I need to do to achieve my goals this week:
___
___
___
___

☆ The long-term goals that I'll work on this week are:
___
___
___

This is what I need to do to work towards them:
___
___
___

☆ This week I'll keep trying to get better at _____ and work on _____
___
___

Pick the goal you want to achieve the most this week and write it here:

Draw one of your goals for this week. Draw what you look like achieving it:

☆ Last week in review:

What were my successes? What goals did I achieve? What can I learn from my successes?

_____

_____

Any mistakes? What can I do differently next time? Can I talk to anyone and ask them questions about how to do better next time (find our their secrets to success)?

_____

_____

Color a star for each goal you achieved last week and write the name of the goal in (draw more stars if you need to):

My plan for the week

☆ Things that I plan to accomplish this week (my short-term goals):
_____
_____
_____

This is what I need to do to achieve my goals this week:
_____
_____
_____
_____

☆ The long-term goals that I'll work on this week are:
_____
_____
_____

This is what I need to do to work towards them:
_____
_____
_____
_____

☆ This week I'll keep trying to get better at _____ and work on _____
_____
_____

Pick the goal you want to achieve the most this week and write it here:

Draw one of your goals for this week. Draw what you look like achieving it:

☆ **Last week in review:**

What were my successes? What goals did I achieve? What can I learn from my successes?

_____

_____

Any mistakes? What can I do differently next time? Can I talk to anyone and ask them questions about how to do better next time (find our their secrets to success)?

_____

_____

Color a star for each goal you achieved last week and write the name of the goal in (draw more stars if you need to):

My plan for the week

☆ Things that I plan to accomplish this week (my short-term goals):
_____
_____
_____

This is what I need to do to achieve my goals this week:
_____
_____
_____
_____

☆ The long-term goals that I'll work on this week are:
_____
_____
_____

This is what I need to do to work towards them:
_____
_____
_____
_____

☆ This week I'll keep trying to get better at _____ and work on _____
_____
_____

Pick the goal you want to achieve the most this week and write it here:

Draw one of your goals for this week. Draw what you look like achieving it:

☆ **Last week in review:**

What were my successes? What goals did I achieve? What can I learn from my successes?

_____
_____

Any mistakes? What can I do differently next time? Can I talk to anyone and ask them questions about how to do better next time (find our their secrets to success)?

_____
_____

Color a star for each goal you achieved last week and write the name of the goal in (draw more stars if you need to):

My plan for the week

☆ Things that I plan to accomplish this week (my short-term goals):
_____
_____
_____

This is what I need to do to achieve my goals this week:
_____
_____
_____
_____

☆ The long-term goals that I'll work on this week are:
_____
_____
_____

This is what I need to do to work towards them:
_____
_____
_____

☆ This week I'll keep trying to get better at _____ and work on _____
_____
_____

Pick the goal you want to achieve the most this week and write it here:

Draw one of your goals for this week. Draw what you look like achieving it:

☆ **Last week in review:**

What were my successes? What goals did I achieve? What can I learn from my successes?

_____
_____

Any mistakes? What can I do differently next time? Can I talk to anyone and ask them questions about how to do better next time (find our their secrets to success)?

_____
_____

Color a star for each goal you achieved last week and write the name of the goal in (draw more stars if you need to):

My plan for the week

☆ Things that I plan to accomplish this week (my short-term goals):
_____
_____
_____

This is what I need to do to achieve my goals this week:
_____
_____
_____
_____

☆ The long-term goals that I'll work on this week are:
_____
_____
_____

This is what I need to do to work towards them:
_____
_____
_____
_____

☆ This week I'll keep trying to get better at _____ and work on _____
_____
_____

Pick the goal you want to achieve the most this week and write it here:

Draw one of your goals for this week. Draw what you look like achieving it:

☆ **Last week in review:**

What were my successes? What goals did I achieve? What can I learn from my successes?

_____
_____

Any mistakes? What can I do differently next time? Can I talk to anyone and ask them questions about how to do better next time (find our their secrets to success)?

_____
_____

Color a star for each goal you achieved last week and write the name of the goal in (draw more stars if you need to):

Let's play a game! Today you're going to build your ideal **tree house.**

What are you going to use to make your tree house?

_____   _____
_____   _____
_____   _____

Does it have any special features?

_____   _____
_____   _____
_____   _____

What do you want to have inside it?

_____   _____
_____   _____
_____   _____

Does it have a secret location?   ☐ Yes   ☐ No

Where? _____

Does it have a secret code to get in? What is it? _____

Every great house has a special name. What are you going to name yours?

Is anyone else allowed in it? _____

Draw your tree house and all its special features:

My plan for the week

☆ Things that I plan to accomplish this week (my short-term goals):
_____
_____
_____

This is what I need to do to achieve my goals this week:
_____
_____
_____
_____

☆ The long-term goals that I'll work on this week are:
_____
_____
_____

This is what I need to do to work towards them:
_____
_____
_____
_____

☆ This week I'll keep trying to get better at _____ and work on _____
_____
_____

Pick the goal you want to achieve the most this week and write it here:

Draw one of your goals for this week. Draw what you look like achieving it:

☆ Last week in review:

What were my successes? What goals did I achieve? What can I learn from my successes?

_____
_____

Any mistakes? What can I do differently next time? Can I talk to anyone and ask them questions about how to do better next time (find our their secrets to success)?

_____
_____

Color a star for each goal you achieved last week and write the name of the goal in (draw more stars if you need to):

My plan for the week

☆ Things that I plan to accomplish this week (my short-term goals):
___
___
___

This is what I need to do to achieve my goals this week:
___
___
___
___

☆ The long-term goals that I'll work on this week are:
___
___
___

This is what I need to do to work towards them:
___
___
___
___

☆ This week I'll keep trying to get better at _____ and work on _____
___
___
___

Pick the goal you want to achieve the most this week and write it here:

Draw one of your goals for this week. Draw what you look like achieving it:

☆ **Last week in review:**

What were my successes? What goals did I achieve? What can I learn from my successes?

_____
_____

Any mistakes? What can I do differently next time? Can I talk to anyone and ask them questions about how to do better next time (find our their secrets to success)?

_____
_____

Color a star for each goal you achieved last week and write the name of the goal in (draw more stars if you need to):

My plan for the week

☆ Things that I plan to accomplish this week (my short-term goals):
_____
_____
_____

This is what I need to do to achieve my goals this week:
_____
_____
_____
_____

☆ The long-term goals that I'll work on this week are:
_____
_____
_____

This is what I need to do to work towards them:
_____
_____
_____
_____

☆ This week I'll keep trying to get better at _____ and work on _____
_____
_____

Pick the goal you want to achieve the most this week and write it here:

Draw one of your goals for this week. Draw what you look like achieving it:

☆ **Last week in review:**

What were my successes? What goals did I achieve? What can I learn from my successes?

_____
_____

Any mistakes? What can I do differently next time? Can I talk to anyone and ask them questions about how to do better next time (find our their secrets to success)?

_____
_____

Color a star for each goal you achieved last week and write the name of the goal in (draw more stars if you need to):

My plan for the week

☆ Things that I plan to accomplish this week (my short-term goals):
_____
_____
_____

This is what I need to do to achieve my goals this week:
_____
_____
_____
_____

☆ The long-term goals that I'll work on this week are:
_____
_____
_____

This is what I need to do to work towards them:
_____
_____
_____
_____

☆ This week I'll keep trying to get better at _____ and work on _____
_____
_____

Pick the goal you want to achieve the most this week and write it here:

Draw one of your goals for this week. Draw what you look like achieving it:

☆ Last week in review:

What were my successes? What goals did I achieve? What can I learn from my successes?

_____

_____

Any mistakes? What can I do differently next time? Can I talk to anyone and ask them questions about how to do better next time (find our their secrets to success)?

_____

_____

Color a star for each goal you achieved last week and write the name of the goal in (draw more stars if you need to):

My plan for the week

☆ Things that I plan to accomplish this week (my short-term goals):
_____
_____
_____

This is what I need to do to achieve my goals this week:
_____
_____
_____
_____

☆ The long-term goals that I'll work on this week are:
_____
_____
_____

This is what I need to do to work towards them:
_____
_____
_____
_____

☆ This week I'll keep trying to get better at _____ and work on _____
_____
_____
_____

Pick the goal you want to achieve the most this week and write it here:

Draw one of your goals for this week. Draw what you look like achieving it:

☆ Last week in review:

What were my successes? What goals did I achieve? What can I learn from my successes?

_____
_____

Any mistakes? What can I do differently next time? Can I talk to anyone and ask them questions about how to do better next time (find our their secrets to success)?

_____
_____

Color a star for each goal you achieved last week and write the name of the goal in (draw more stars if you need to):

My plan for the week

☆ Things that I plan to accomplish this week (my short-term goals):
_____
_____
_____

This is what I need to do to achieve my goals this week:
_____
_____
_____

☆ The long-term goals that I'll work on this week are:
_____
_____
_____

This is what I need to do to work towards them:
_____
_____
_____

☆ This week I'll keep trying to get better at _____ and work on _____
_____
_____

Pick the goal you want to achieve the most this week and write it here:

Draw one of your goals for this week. Draw what you look like achieving it:

☆ Last week in review:

What were my successes? What goals did I achieve? What can I learn from my successes?

_____
_____

Any mistakes? What can I do differently next time? Can I talk to anyone and ask them questions about how to do better next time (find our their secrets to success)?

_____
_____

Color a star for each goal you achieved last week and write the name of the goal in (draw more stars if you need to):

My plan for the week

☆ Things that I plan to accomplish this week (my short-term goals):
___
___
___

This is what I need to do to achieve my goals this week:
___
___
___
___

☆ The long-term goals that I'll work on this week are:
___
___
___

This is what I need to do to work towards them:
___
___
___

☆ This week I'll keep trying to get better at _____ and work on _____
___
___
___

Pick the goal you want to achieve the most this week and write it here:

Draw one of your goals for this week. Draw what you look like achieving it:

☆ **Last week in review:**

What were my successes? What goals did I achieve? What can I learn from my successes?

_____
_____

Any mistakes? What can I do differently next time? Can I talk to anyone and ask them questions about how to do better next time (find our their secrets to success)?

_____
_____

Color a star for each goal you achieved last week and write the name of the goal in (draw more stars if you need to):

Let's play a game! You're going to a place you've **never been to**, but want to go.

Where do you want to go? _____

Why do you want to go there?
_____
_____

How will you get there?
_____
_____

What is the first thing you'll do when you get there?
_____
_____

What are the other things you want to do?

_____ _____
_____ _____
_____ _____

How long will you stay? _____ Years _____ Months _____ Days

What are you going to bring with you?

_____ _____
_____ _____
_____ _____

Are you going to invite anyone to come along with you? Who? _____
_____

Draw this fabulous place. And yourself there.

My plan for the week

☆ Things that I plan to accomplish this week (my short-term goals):
_____
_____
_____

This is what I need to do to achieve my goals this week:
_____
_____
_____
_____

☆ The long-term goals that I'll work on this week are:
_____
_____
_____

This is what I need to do to work towards them:
_____
_____
_____

☆ This week I'll keep trying to get better at _____ and work on _____
_____
_____

Pick the goal you want to achieve the most this week and write it here:

Draw one of your goals for this week. Draw what you look like achieving it:

☆ **Last week in review:**

What were my successes? What goals did I achieve? What can I learn from my successes?

_____
_____

Any mistakes? What can I do differently next time? Can I talk to anyone and ask them questions about how to do better next time (find our their secrets to success)?

_____
_____

Color a star for each goal you achieved last week and write the name of the goal in (draw more stars if you need to):

My plan for the week

☆ Things that I plan to accomplish this week (my short-term goals):
___
___
___

This is what I need to do to achieve my goals this week:
___
___
___
___

☆ The long-term goals that I'll work on this week are:
___
___
___

This is what I need to do to work towards them:
___
___
___
___

☆ This week I'll keep trying to get better at _____ and work on _____
___
___

Pick the goal you want to achieve the most this week and write it here:

Draw one of your goals for this week. Draw what you look like achieving it:

☆ Last week in review:

What were my successes? What goals did I achieve? What can I learn from my successes?

_____

_____

Any mistakes? What can I do differently next time? Can I talk to anyone and ask them questions about how to do better next time (find our their secrets to success)?

_____

_____

Color a star for each goal you achieved last week and write the name of the goal in (draw more stars if you need to):

My plan for the week

☆ Things that I plan to accomplish this week (my short-term goals):
_____
_____
_____

This is what I need to do to achieve my goals this week:
_____
_____
_____
_____

☆ The long-term goals that I'll work on this week are:
_____
_____
_____

This is what I need to do to work towards them:
_____
_____
_____

☆ This week I'll keep trying to get better at _____ and work on _____
_____
_____

Pick the goal you want to achieve the most this week and write it here:

Draw one of your goals for this week. Draw what you look like achieving it:

☆ **Last week in review:**

What were my successes? What goals did I achieve? What can I learn from my successes?

_____
_____

Any mistakes? What can I do differently next time? Can I talk to anyone and ask them questions about how to do better next time (find our their secrets to success)?

_____
_____

Color a star for each goal you achieved last week and write the name of the goal in (draw more stars if you need to):

My plan for the week

☆ Things that I plan to accomplish this week (my short-term goals):
_____
_____
_____

This is what I need to do to achieve my goals this week:
_____
_____
_____
_____

☆ The long-term goals that I'll work on this week are:
_____
_____
_____

This is what I need to do to work towards them:
_____
_____
_____
_____

☆ This week I'll keep trying to get better at _____ and work on _____
_____
_____

Pick the goal you want to achieve the most this week and write it here:

Draw one of your goals for this week. Draw what you look like achieving it:

☆ **Last week in review:**

What were my successes? What goals did I achieve? What can I learn from my successes?

_____

_____

Any mistakes? What can I do differently next time? Can I talk to anyone and ask them questions about how to do better next time (find our their secrets to success)?

_____

_____

Color a star for each goal you achieved last week and write the name of the goal in (draw more stars if you need to):

My plan for the week

☆ Things that I plan to accomplish this week (my short-term goals):
_____
_____
_____

This is what I need to do to achieve my goals this week:
_____
_____
_____
_____

☆ The long-term goals that I'll work on this week are:
_____
_____
_____

This is what I need to do to work towards them:
_____
_____
_____
_____

☆ This week I'll keep trying to get better at _____ and work on _____
_____
_____
_____

Pick the goal you want to achieve the most this week and write it here:

Draw one of your goals for this week. Draw what you look like achieving it:

☆ Last week in review:

What were my successes? What goals did I achieve? What can I learn from my successes?

_____
_____

Any mistakes? What can I do differently next time? Can I talk to anyone and ask them questions about how to do better next time (find our their secrets to success)?

_____
_____

Color a star for each goal you achieved last week and write the name of the goal in (draw more stars if you need to):

My plan for the week

☆ Things that I plan to accomplish this week (my short-term goals):
_____
_____
_____

This is what I need to do to achieve my goals this week:
_____
_____
_____
_____

☆ The long-term goals that I'll work on this week are:
_____
_____
_____

This is what I need to do to work towards them:
_____
_____
_____
_____

☆ This week I'll keep trying to get better at _____ and work on _____
_____
_____

Pick the goal you want to achieve the most this week and write it here:

Draw one of your goals for this week. Draw what you look like achieving it:

☆ Last week in review:

What were my successes? What goals did I achieve? What can I learn from my successes?

_____
_____

Any mistakes? What can I do differently next time? Can I talk to anyone and ask them questions about how to do better next time (find our their secrets to success)?

_____
_____

Color a star for each goal you achieved last week and write the name of the goal in (draw more stars if you need to):

Let's play a game! You've made the **front page** of the newspaper!

What is the headline? _____

Why are they writing about you in the newspaper?
_____
_____

Write the article:
_____
_____
_____
_____
_____
_____
_____
_____
_____
_____
_____
_____
_____
_____
_____
_____
_____
_____
_____
_____

Draw the front page of the newspaper, include the headline and the photo(s) that go with it.

My plan for the week

☆ Things that I plan to accomplish this week (my short-term goals):
_____
_____
_____

This is what I need to do to achieve my goals this week:
_____
_____
_____
_____

☆ The long-term goals that I'll work on this week are:
_____
_____
_____

This is what I need to do to work towards them:
_____
_____
_____
_____

☆ This week I'll keep trying to get better at _____ and work on _____
_____
_____

Pick the goal you want to achieve the most this week and write it here:

Draw one of your goals for this week. Draw what you look like achieving it:

☆ Last week in review:

What were my successes? What goals did I achieve? What can I learn from my successes?

_____
_____

Any mistakes? What can I do differently next time? Can I talk to anyone and ask them questions about how to do better next time (find our their secrets to success)?

_____
_____

Color a star for each goal you achieved last week and write the name of the goal in (draw more stars if you need to):

My plan for the week

☆ Things that I plan to accomplish this week (my short-term goals):
_____
_____
_____

This is what I need to do to achieve my goals this week:
_____
_____
_____
_____

☆ The long-term goals that I'll work on this week are:
_____
_____
_____

This is what I need to do to work towards them:
_____
_____
_____
_____

☆ This week I'll keep trying to get better at _____ and work on _____
_____
_____

Pick the goal you want to achieve the most this week and write it here:

Draw one of your goals for this week. Draw what you look like achieving it:

☆ Last week in review:

What were my successes? What goals did I achieve? What can I learn from my successes?

_____
_____

Any mistakes? What can I do differently next time? Can I talk to anyone and ask them questions about how to do better next time (find our their secrets to success)?

_____
_____

Color a star for each goal you achieved last week and write the name of the goal in (draw more stars if you need to):

My plan for the week

☆ Things that I plan to accomplish this week (my short-term goals):
_____
_____
_____

This is what I need to do to achieve my goals this week:
_____
_____
_____
_____

☆ The long-term goals that I'll work on this week are:
_____
_____
_____

This is what I need to do to work towards them:
_____
_____
_____
_____

☆ This week I'll keep trying to get better at _____ and work on _____
_____
_____

Pick the goal you want to achieve the most this week and write it here:

Draw one of your goals for this week. Draw what you look like achieving it:

☆ Last week in review:

What were my successes? What goals did I achieve? What can I learn from my successes?

_____
_____

Any mistakes? What can I do differently next time? Can I talk to anyone and ask them questions about how to do better next time (find our their secrets to success)?

_____
_____

Color a star for each goal you achieved last week and write the name of the goal in (draw more stars if you need to):

My plan for the week

☆ Things that I plan to accomplish this week (my short-term goals):
___
___
___

This is what I need to do to achieve my goals this week:
___
___
___
___

☆ The long-term goals that I'll work on this week are:
___
___
___

This is what I need to do to work towards them:
___
___
___
___

☆ This week I'll keep trying to get better at _____ and work on _____
___
___
___

Pick the goal you want to achieve the most this week and write it here:

Draw one of your goals for this week. Draw what you look like achieving it:

☆ Last week in review:

What were my successes? What goals did I achieve? What can I learn from my successes?

_____
_____

Any mistakes? What can I do differently next time? Can I talk to anyone and ask them questions about how to do better next time (find our their secrets to success)?

_____
_____

Color a star for each goal you achieved last week and write the name of the goal in (draw more stars if you need to):

My plan for the week

☆ Things that I plan to accomplish this week (my short-term goals):
_____
_____
_____

This is what I need to do to achieve my goals this week:
_____
_____
_____
_____

☆ The long-term goals that I'll work on this week are:
_____
_____
_____

This is what I need to do to work towards them:
_____
_____
_____
_____

☆ This week I'll keep trying to get better at _____ and work on _____
_____
_____

Pick the goal you want to achieve the most this week and write it here:

Draw one of your goals for this week. Draw what you look like achieving it:

☆ Last week in review:

What were my successes? What goals did I achieve? What can I learn from my successes?

_____
_____

Any mistakes? What can I do differently next time? Can I talk to anyone and ask them questions about how to do better next time (find our their secrets to success)?

_____
_____

Color a star for each goal you achieved last week and write the name of the goal in (draw more stars if you need to):

My plan for the week

☆ Things that I plan to accomplish this week (my short-term goals):
_____
_____
_____

This is what I need to do to achieve my goals this week:
_____
_____
_____

☆ The long-term goals that I'll work on this week are:
_____
_____
_____

This is what I need to do to work towards them:
_____
_____
_____

☆ This week I'll keep trying to get better at _____ and work on _____
_____
_____

Pick the goal you want to achieve the most this week and write it here:

Draw one of your goals for this week. Draw what you look like achieving it:

☆ Last week in review:

What were my successes? What goals did I achieve? What can I learn from my successes?

_____
_____

Any mistakes? What can I do differently next time? Can I talk to anyone and ask them questions about how to do better next time (find our their secrets to success)?

_____
_____

Color a star for each goal you achieved last week and write the name of the goal in (draw more stars if you need to):

Let's play a game! You're a **great explorer**.

What kind of an explorer are you? _____

What are your special skills?

_____   _____

_____   _____

Where do you want to go exploring?

_____

_____

What continent is that on? Or is it on a different planet? _____

What equipment will you bring with you?

_____   _____

_____   _____

Will you have a team of explorers with you or will you be exploring by yourself?

_____

_____

What are some of your discoveries? Give them some interesting names:

_____   _____

_____   _____

Draw yourself making your greatest discovery. Or draw a map of your expedition:

My plan for the week

☆ Things that I plan to accomplish this week (my short-term goals):
_____
_____
_____

This is what I need to do to achieve my goals this week:
_____
_____
_____
_____

☆ The long-term goals that I'll work on this week are:
_____
_____
_____

This is what I need to do to work towards them:
_____
_____
_____
_____

☆ This week I'll keep trying to get better at _____ and work on _____
_____
_____

Pick the goal you want to achieve the most this week and write it here:

Draw one of your goals for this week. Draw what you look like achieving it:

☆ **Last week in review:**

What were my successes? What goals did I achieve? What can I learn from my successes?

_____

_____

Any mistakes? What can I do differently next time? Can I talk to anyone and ask them questions about how to do better next time (find our their secrets to success)?

_____

_____

Color a star for each goal you achieved last week and write the name of the goal in (draw more stars if you need to):

My plan for the week

☆ Things that I plan to accomplish this week (my short-term goals):
_____
_____
_____

This is what I need to do to achieve my goals this week:
_____
_____
_____
_____

☆ The long-term goals that I'll work on this week are:
_____
_____
_____

This is what I need to do to work towards them:
_____
_____
_____
_____

☆ This week I'll keep trying to get better at _____ and work on _____
_____
_____

Pick the goal you want to achieve the most this week and write it here:

Draw one of your goals for this week. Draw what you look like achieving it:

☆ Last week in review:

What were my successes? What goals did I achieve? What can I learn from my successes?

_____
_____

Any mistakes? What can I do differently next time? Can I talk to anyone and ask them questions about how to do better next time (find our their secrets to success)?

_____
_____

Color a star for each goal you achieved last week and write the name of the goal in (draw more stars if you need to):

My plan for the week

☆ Things that I plan to accomplish this week (my short-term goals):
_____
_____
_____

This is what I need to do to achieve my goals this week:
_____
_____
_____

☆ The long-term goals that I'll work on this week are:
_____
_____
_____

This is what I need to do to work towards them:
_____
_____
_____

☆ This week I'll keep trying to get better at _____ and work on _____
_____
_____

Pick the goal you want to achieve the most this week and write it here:

Draw one of your goals for this week. Draw what you look like achieving it:

☆ **Last week in review:**

What were my successes? What goals did I achieve? What can I learn from my successes?

_____

_____

Any mistakes? What can I do differently next time? Can I talk to anyone and ask them questions about how to do better next time (find our their secrets to success)?

_____

_____

Color a star for each goal you achieved last week and write the name of the goal in (draw more stars if you need to):

My plan for the week

☆ Things that I plan to accomplish this week (my short-term goals):
_____
_____
_____

This is what I need to do to achieve my goals this week:
_____
_____
_____
_____

☆ The long-term goals that I'll work on this week are:
_____
_____
_____

This is what I need to do to work towards them:
_____
_____
_____
_____

☆ This week I'll keep trying to get better at _____ and work on _____
_____
_____
_____

Pick the goal you want to achieve the most this week and write it here:

Draw one of your goals for this week. Draw what you look like achieving it:

☆ Last week in review:

What were my successes? What goals did I achieve? What can I learn from my successes?

_____
_____

Any mistakes? What can I do differently next time? Can I talk to anyone and ask them questions about how to do better next time (find our their secrets to success)?

_____
_____

Color a star for each goal you achieved last week and write the name of the goal in (draw more stars if you need to):

My plan for the week

☆ Things that I plan to accomplish this week (my short-term goals):
___
___
___

This is what I need to do to achieve my goals this week:
___
___
___
___

☆ The long-term goals that I'll work on this week are:
___
___
___

This is what I need to do to work towards them:
___
___
___

☆ This week I'll keep trying to get better at _____ and work on _____
___
___

Pick the goal you want to achieve the most this week and write it here:

Draw one of your goals for this week. Draw what you look like achieving it:

☆ Last week in review:

What were my successes? What goals did I achieve? What can I learn from my successes?

_____

_____

Any mistakes? What can I do differently next time? Can I talk to anyone and ask them questions about how to do better next time (find our their secrets to success)?

_____

_____

Color a star for each goal you achieved last week and write the name of the goal in (draw more stars if you need to):

My plan for the week

☆ Things that I plan to accomplish this week (my short-term goals):
_____
_____
_____

This is what I need to do to achieve my goals this week:
_____
_____
_____
_____

☆ The long-term goals that I'll work on this week are:
_____
_____
_____

This is what I need to do to work towards them:
_____
_____
_____
_____

☆ This week I'll keep trying to get better at _____ and work on _____
_____
_____

Pick the goal you want to achieve the most this week and write it here:

Draw one of your goals for this week. Draw what you look like achieving it:

☆ **Last week in review:**

What were my successes? What goals did I achieve? What can I learn from my successes?

_____
_____

Any mistakes? What can I do differently next time? Can I talk to anyone and ask them questions about how to do better next time (find our their secrets to success)?

_____
_____

Color a star for each goal you achieved last week and write the name of the goal in (draw more stars if you need to):

Let's play a game! Imagine you **wrote a book**.

What is the title of your book?

What is it about?
_____
_____

Is it a long book?   ☐ Yes   ☐ No

How long did it take you to write it? _____ Years _____ Months _____ Days

How did you get the idea for the book?
_____
_____

Who are the main characters in your book?

_____   _____
_____   _____

What are some of the most exciting things that happen in the book?
_____
_____

Think of the most boring book you've ever read. How can you make it better and more interesting?
_____
_____

Draw the cover of your book.

My plan for the week

☆ Things that I plan to accomplish this week (my short-term goals):
_____
_____
_____

This is what I need to do to achieve my goals this week:
_____
_____
_____
_____

☆ The long-term goals that I'll work on this week are:
_____
_____
_____

This is what I need to do to work towards them:
_____
_____
_____
_____

☆ This week I'll keep trying to get better at _____ and work on _____
_____
_____

Pick the goal you want to achieve the most this week and write it here:

Draw one of your goals for this week. Draw what you look like achieving it:

☆ Last week in review:

What were my successes? What goals did I achieve? What can I learn from my successes?

_____

_____

Any mistakes? What can I do differently next time? Can I talk to anyone and ask them questions about how to do better next time (find our their secrets to success)?

_____

_____

Color a star for each goal you achieved last week and write the name of the goal in (draw more stars if you need to):

My plan for the week

☆ Things that I plan to accomplish this week (my short-term goals):
_____
_____
_____

This is what I need to do to achieve my goals this week:
_____
_____
_____
_____

☆ The long-term goals that I'll work on this week are:
_____
_____
_____

This is what I need to do to work towards them:
_____
_____
_____
_____

☆ This week I'll keep trying to get better at _____ and work on _____
_____
_____

Pick the goal you want to achieve the most this week and write it here:

Draw one of your goals for this week. Draw what you look like achieving it:

☆ Last week in review:

What were my successes? What goals did I achieve? What can I learn from my successes?

_____
_____

Any mistakes? What can I do differently next time? Can I talk to anyone and ask them questions about how to do better next time (find our their secrets to success)?

_____
_____

Color a star for each goal you achieved last week and write the name of the goal in (draw more stars if you need to):

My plan for the week

☆ Things that I plan to accomplish this week (my short-term goals):
_____
_____
_____

This is what I need to do to achieve my goals this week:
_____
_____
_____
_____

☆ The long-term goals that I'll work on this week are:
_____
_____
_____

This is what I need to do to work towards them:
_____
_____
_____
_____

☆ This week I'll keep trying to get better at _____ and work on _____
_____
_____

Pick the goal you want to achieve the most this week and write it here:

Draw one of your goals for this week. Draw what you look like achieving it:

☆ Last week in review:

What were my successes? What goals did I achieve? What can I learn from my successes?

_____

_____

Any mistakes? What can I do differently next time? Can I talk to anyone and ask them questions about how to do better next time (find our their secrets to success)?

_____

_____

Color a star for each goal you achieved last week and write the name of the goal in (draw more stars if you need to):

Made in United States
North Haven, CT
27 March 2024

50545267R00076